BLACKOUT

Jeff Gottesfeld

SADDLEBACK
EDUCATIONAL PUBLISHING

red rhino
b**OO**k s®

SADDLEBACK
EDUCATIONAL PUBLISHING
www.sdlback.com

ISBN-13: 978-1-62250-956-0
ISBN-10: 1-62250-956-0
eBook: 978-1-63078-179-8

Printed in Malaysia

20 19 18 17 16   1 2 3 4 5

Ellie

Age: 12

Favorite Subject: art history

Likes: playing the piano

Dislikes: practicing the piano

Best Quality: is not jealous of her friends

CHARACTERS

Nana and Poppa

Combined Age: 132

Favorite Hobby: flipping houses

Biggest Secret: went to Woodstock

Special Talent: calligraphy

Best Quality: believe in free-range parenting

1

STORM WARNING

Ellie looked out the living room window. Her grandparents' cottage was right on the beach. The window faced the sand. The blue ocean was past that. Seabirds painted the sky. Puffy clouds hung to the west.

It was ten in the morning. The beach was already crowded. Ocean Grove was a great place to come in the summer.

Ellie and her friend Kate flew in the day before. They lived in Texas. It was Ellie's first trip without her parents. She had begged for years to visit her grandparents by herself. She would begin seventh grade soon. So her mom and dad said she was ready.

The girls would be there for a week. They got in after sunset. This was their first real day.

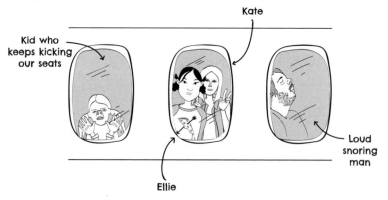

Kate

Kid who keeps kicking our seats

Loud snoring man

Ellie

"Hey!" Kate called.

"What's up?" Ellie asked. "Want to go to the beach?"

"Not yet. Check this out. Jordan just 'liked' our pic from the plane. We have 95 'likes.' That's the most ever!"

♥ ● ↱   ♥95
Long Plane Ride!
@kate #springbreak
@kate You guys look cool ✌

Ellie turned and grinned. She and Kate loved social media. They texted all day long. Both girls had smartphones. Kate even slept with hers. She checked it first thing in the morning. Last thing at night too.

"That's great," Ellie said. "Can you find him on chat?"

"Let me see. It's two hours later back home. Got him!"

Ellie joined Kate on the couch. Kate held up her phone. There was Jordan. His grin filled the screen. He was a fine guy. Ellie knew that Kate liked him. Like, *liked him*. They were an epic pair.

Ellie thought Kate was perfect. She had blonde hair and blue eyes. She looked super pretty in all of her selfies. She took *a lot* of them.

♥ 🗨 ⌐⁵⁰
Chillin'

♥ 🗨 ⌐⁶⁷
Just Me!

♥ 🗨 ⌐⁴²
Trying on Shades

"What's up?" Jordan asked.

"Nothing much. What's up with you?" Kate asked him.

"Not much. Hanging out. Maybe going to the waterpark with Pete. It's hot here."

"That's cool," Ellie said. This was not a very fun talk. She hoped they would go to the beach soon. She came to Ocean Grove to swim. Spend time with her grandparents. Not to chat with boys back home.

"Um, girls?" Ellie's grandma stood in the doorway. Everyone called her Nana. Ellie's grandpa was called Poppa. "Can I have a word?"

"Sure, Nana. Kate, try Jordan later. Okay?" Ellie asked.

"You got it." Kate clicked off. They sat with Ellie's grandma. Nana was a great lady. She had more energy than a lot of kids.

Poppa was cool too. He loved to read. He could build stuff. In the garage there was a woodshop. There was every tool ever made. Lots of old stuff as well.

"Two things," Nana said. "First I want you girls to go outside. It's too nice to be inside."

"But there are no bars!" Kate moaned. "I checked when we got here."

Nana looked at her oddly. "Bars? You can't drink. You're twelve years old!"

Ellie smiled. Her Nana didn't get it.

"Kate means bars on her cell phone. So she can use it."

"You're at the beach," Nana said. "Forget the phones. Go have fun."

"Phones are fun," Kate said.

Nana shook her head. "You both are too young for those darn things. When I was your age—oh, forget it. One more thing. I heard the news this morning. There will be a solar storm today. It may hit in France. Be glad it's not here."

♥ 💬 ↱   ♥25k
BREAKING NEWS!
#solarstorm

Ellie knew what a solar storm was. She had studied them last year. The sun had dark spots. Those spots sent out waves. Not ocean waves. Energy waves. If the waves were too strong, they could knock out power. There had been a bad solar storm in Canada. That had been some years ago. It had knocked out the power in some big towns.

"I'm glad we're not in France," Ellie said. She was ready to swim. "Come on, Kate. Let's go to the beach."

Kate smiled. "What? And not get texts?"

Ellie bopped her with a pillow. "You'll live."

Kate fell back against the couch. Then she looked sadly at her cell phone. "Goodbye, dear phone. I'll miss you!"

2

SOLAR STORM

It was the next morning. Ellie was the first one up. She dressed and made her bed. The day before had been so much fun. She and Kate had been at the beach. They posted a ton of pictures. Some of cute guys. Some of waves. And lots of selfies.

♥ ☺ r* ♥50
Hot #iheartboys☺

♥ ☺ r* ♥67
Nice Swell! ✍

♥ ☺ r* ♥42
☺ #selfiesaturday

Ellie made her bed. Then she checked

9

her phone. Many comments had come in overnight. But then they had stopped. That was at about three in the morning. She could not see her "likes." None of her web apps loaded. Her phone had no bars at all. That was weird.

The light didn't work in the bathroom. The strangest thing? Her phone wasn't fully charged. She had plugged it in when she went to sleep. She always did. That way she didn't have to worry about it all day. But it was not at 100 percent.

She plugged it in again. Nope. No power coming in. She checked Kate's phone. Same thing. Then she tried the lights in the hall. Nothing.

Whoa! No doubt about it. The power was out.

She heard a sound in the kitchen. Ellie walked over. Poppa drank coffee at the table. He had a small radio. The volume was turned low.

Poppa likes his coffee black

"Big news," he told her.

"Is it a blackout? I think the power is out."

"Yes. A big one. It's that solar storm. Kind of a shock. It hit here. Everything is down and out. Power. TV. Cell phones."

Ellie's eyes got big. "For how long?"

Her grandfather tapped the radio. "I'm listening to the news. The station has backup power. My radio has a crank. Wait. Shhh. Good news. The blackout is not for long. They say the power will be back on by tonight. They have to work on the grid. They want people off the roads. The crews have to move."

Ellie grinned. "Phew! That's good. A

super long blackout would be a bad thing."

The day turned out okay. The girls went to the beach for a while. They flew kites. There was plenty to eat. Poppa lit the grill. She and Kate had games on their phones. They played the games. Looked at pictures. Read old texts.

Nana and Poppa kept them up on the news. Power was out down much of the coast. There were a lot of crews working. The rest of the country was okay.

The only bad thing was their phones. They got low on juice. It was a good thing the power was coming on soon. Ellie did not want to go a night without her smartphone. She would feel so alone.

3

DARKNESS

It was dark. Power was still out. There was light in the dining room. But it came from candles. Ellie and Kate were on the couch. The old folks were in two chairs.

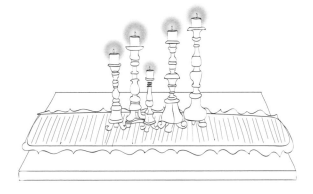

They drank warm sodas. The fridge and freezer were kept closed. The food needed to stay cold. That would work for a day or two. Then they would need ice.

It was heating up, though. Ocean Grove was almost always cool. But not that night. The forecast was for more of the same. All the windows were open. The cottage was still stuffy.

"This reminds me of when I was working in New York," Nana said.

"The blackout of 1968?" Poppa asked.

"That was the one. I lived on the 15th floor.

It was in a building near Times Square. I had to climb the stairs to get home. And walk home from work too. The subways weren't running. The streets were so jammed up," Nana said. "That was quite a time."

"What did you do all night?" Ellie asked.

"Nothing much. People were very nice. We met on the street. Shared food and water. We just waited for the lights to come back on."

Poppa nodded. His face looked funny

in the candlelight. "You know, girls, folks lived a long time without lights. Take my grandparents—"

"What time is it?" Kate asked.

Poppa had an old watch. The kind that wound up. That's how he could tell the time. "Well, it's getting close to nine. Let's listen to the news." He moved to the radio. Flicked it on. The news had started.

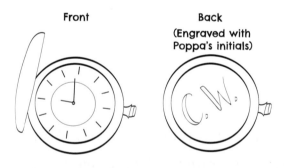

Front

Back
(Engraved with Poppa's initials)

"We are working hard to get the power on. But there are more problems with the grid. There's no telling how long you'll be in the dark. There are extra police patrols. Water, food, and ice too," said the radio voice. "The army will bring out anyone sick or injured. So far, people have been great. Let's keep it that way. Stay tuned for more news every hour on the hour. That's all."

Poppa turned off the radio. "Well, we're in it now."

Ellie and Kate looked at each other.

"You scared?" Ellie asked.

Kate shook her head. "Nope. Not scared. Bored. If this goes on for a while? I could be bored to death. I miss my phone. Maybe I'm addicted to it."

Everyone laughed.

"You've never been in a blackout?" Nana asked.

Kate nodded. "Maybe for an hour. When there's been a big storm."

"There was that ice storm," Ellie

reminded her. "The power was out all day. School was closed."

"That's right. Worst day of my life."

Everyone laughed again. Poppa went and opened the door. "I don't think we need to worry about being robbed."

It was so hot. The open door did not help much. The breeze off the ocean just moved the air a little. It was going to be a long, hot night.

4

BOREDOM

It took a long time to get to sleep. The bedroom was too hot. Nana told the girls to soak washcloths in water. Ellie and Kate draped the cloths on their faces. That helped a little.

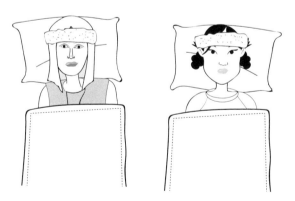

It was no better in the morning. The day

was even hotter. Breakfast was bread and peanut butter. And water. Nana and Poppa had been smart. They had filled buckets with water. The water came out slowly from the faucet. There was no telling how long it would stay on.

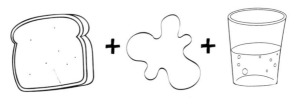

Blackout Breakfast

"I don't know why we don't just go home," Kate said. She wiped the crumbs off her plate. Washing it would waste water. "Let's go where there's power."

Poppa shook his head. "Can't do it. Most roads are closed. If we run out of gas, we're stuck. It takes power to pump gas."

"So many things need power," Ellie said.

Nana smiled. "Not our feet. We should walk to town. See what's up. Maybe we can find some ice."

Probably already melted

ICE

"Good idea," Kate told her. "There's nothing to do here."

"There's the beach. The water is great," Nana said.

Kate sighed. "Know what I miss?"

"What?" Nana asked.

"My phone!"

Thirty minutes later, they walked to

town. There were no cars. People stood in the street. Kids ran and played. Some teens tossed a ball.

Main Street was four blocks long. There were stores on both sides. A few were open. Most of the food was gone. The owners only took cash. There were still big lines. There was no ice at all. It was sold out.

"Are we okay for food?" Ellie asked Nana.

"We have lots," Nana said. "Money too. There's a safe in the bedroom."

It was a good thing. There was a bank on Main Street. It had an ATM. A long line of people waited outside it. Ellie thought that was odd. The ATM needed power. But the power was out. Why was anyone waiting?

Ellie went to a teen girl in line. She looked about 16. And wow, she had a great tan! The girl was playing cards with some other people.

"Why are you waiting?" Ellie asked the girl. "The ATM isn't working. Right?"

"Right."

"Then why—"

"Because I'm broke, that's why." The girl

shrugged. "When it comes back on, I want to use it. Before it runs out of money."

"You could be here a long time," Kate said.

"Tell me about it," the girl told them. "Hey. It's not so bad. The cops are bringing food. And water. And it isn't raining."

"Good luck," Ellie said.

They walked over to the ocean. There were some people on the beach, but not many. The games on the boardwalk were closed. No power. No food or drinks. No music. No parking lots full of cars.

Then they walked back to the cottage. Ellie thought about her mom and dad. She had not talked to them. There was no way. They had to be upset.

When they were home, she went to Poppa.

"Poppa?"

"Yeah?"

"My parents must be going nuts."

He nodded. "Could be. But you have to wait to call them."

"I don't want to wait." Ellie felt a little sick.

Helicopter parents, LOL!

MISSING

He smiled oddly. "Well then. Know what? Maybe you don't have to wait."

"What do you mean?"

He pointed to the front door. "Let's try Plan B. Go get Kate. And meet me in 10 minutes."

5

HAM

The house looked like a junk shop.

There were tools on the porch. A rusted car was parked on the lawn. The windows were all shut. Long wires came out of the sidewall. They ran up a tall tree. Ellie heard a loud motor. It seemed to be running out back.

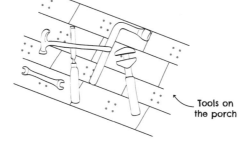

Tools on the porch

Ellie and Kate had walked over. Nana

and Poppa were with them. Ellie turned to Poppa.

"This place is okay?"

He laughed. "It's fine."

"It looks like a movie set," Ellie said.

"Yeah," Kate agreed. "For a slasher movie!"

Poppa chuckled. "I don't think so. What do you say, Nana?"

Odd duck?

"It's fine," Nana said. "Homer's just an odd duck. I'll bet he's home. Homer is always home." She smacked the knocker against the front door. It was an old bone tied to a rope.

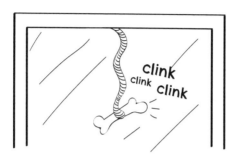

The door swung open. A man stood there. He looked young. Younger than Ellie's parents, for sure. He wore gym shorts. An old T-shirt. He had short hair. His beard was long. It looked scruffy. But the man had a huge smile.

"Carl and Martha!" he said. "And two kids. Come on it!"

Ellie stepped inside. The lights were all on. It was cool inside. Even cold. Which had to mean …

"You have power!" Ellie shouted.

"I do. Yes. You heard the engine out back," Homer said. "It runs on gas. That gives me power. But I don't use it all the time. You're lucky to show up now."

Poppa looked at Ellie. "Tell Homer why we're here."

Ellie cleared her throat. "Well … my grandpa says you can help Kate and me. We want to talk to our parents. They're in Texas. But I don't get how you can do that. You have power, sure. But landlines are all out. Right?"

"And the cell towers," Kate added.

Homer grinned. "True. But I am a ham."

"You're a what?"

Ellie didn't get it.

Kate was mixed up too. "A ham? Like, you're an actor? You ham it up?"

"Not exactly." Homer crooked his finger. He pointed toward the back of his place. "Follow me."

Homer led them to a back room. His place was a mess. There were piles of books. The lightbulbs were all bare.

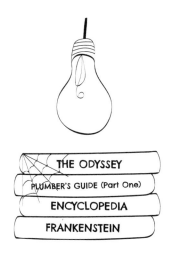

THE ODYSSEY
PLUMBER'S GUIDE (Part One)
ENCYCLOPEDIA
FRANKENSTEIN

Ellie didn't care. She just wanted to talk to her parents.

All five people crowded into the room. It had no windows. The floor was bare wood.

Radio gear was everywhere. Wires ran out a hole in one wall.

Homer sat at a table. He put on some headphones. Then he turned some knobs. There were big speakers. Static filled the air.

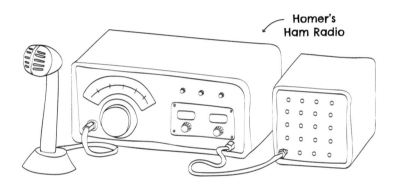

Homer's Ham Radio

"This is called a ham radio," Homer said. "I use it to talk to people far away."

"Why don't you just call them by phone?" Kate asked.

"I do. But this is more fun. And you can't call when the phones are down. Where did you say you're from?"

Ellie told him the name of their Texas town.

"Stand by," Homer said.

He got on the radio. He reached a friend in Kansas. The phones worked fine there. Then he got the girls' home numbers. His friend stayed on the radio with Homer. And he called Ellie's house on his phone.

A moment later Ellie was talking to her parents. She talked into Homer's radio mic. The man in Kansas had his phone on speaker. Her folks in Texas heard her on their phone.

"I'm fine," she told them. "Nana and Poppa are the best!"

"You stay safe," her mother told her. "Thank the nice man with the radio."

Ellie was done. Then Kate got to talk to her mom too. When they were done, they

35

thanked Homer over and over. He said they could come back anytime.

One big worry was gone.

All that was left was to be hot. And bored.

6

THE TRUNK

"I'm too old for this," Nana said.

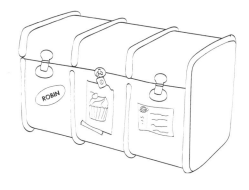

Ellie's grandma put down one end of a big trunk. There was a coating of gray dust on top. They all had lugged it in from the garage. Poppa had seen how bored the kids were. He said maybe the trunk could help.

It took a few moments to wipe off all the dust. Then Nana looked at Poppa. "I think I'll go read."

"I think I'll join you." He turned to the kids. "We'll leave this with you."

"Don't you want to see what's in it?" Ellie asked.

Poppa smiled. "We've had that trunk forever. We know what's inside. Have fun."

The old folks left. The girls were alone with the trunk. Ellie eyed it. There was a small lock on it. The lock was open.

"What do you think?" Kate asked.

"I think we just talked to our parents. Now we're bored to death. Nana and Poppa said there's good stuff in here. Let's look."

They opened the trunk. Poppa was right. It was full of good stuff.

There were playing cards. Board games.

Books. A kit for something called a crystal radio. Old clothes. Notebooks and pens. School yearbooks. Boxes of photos. Music albums. Nothing was less than 30 years old. Some of it was far older.

Kate held up one of the albums. It was from a band called Depeche Mode. Ellie knew the band. "My mom and dad listen to these guys!"

They spent the next two hours going through the stuff. The sun set, so they lit candles. Ellie loved the crystal radio. It was a radio you could make from a kit. It needed no power. She wrapped wire around a coil. Then she added some other parts. Finally she wired on an old earphone.

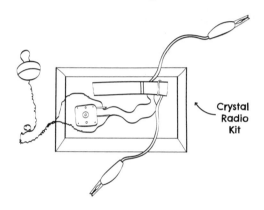

Crystal Radio Kit

"Does that thing work?" Kate asked.

"Let's see."

Ellie put the earphone in her ear. To her shock, she heard a news report.

"The power will be back on soon. Again, stay calm. Stay off the roads. Help is coming."

Her face shined. "It works. You don't need power to have a radio. Listen."

Kate tried. Her face lit up. "Wow! It does work."

While Kate kept listening, Ellie checked out the books. One was called *Love Story*. There was a cute guy and girl on the cover. It looked good. Maybe she would take it back to Texas.

Back to Texas

Next she opened one of the notebooks. It had a clasp. The notebook had pink paper. It was filled with writing. She knew whose writing it was. Her mother's!

She read the first page. The date was from May. It was in the early 1990s. There were many pages. They were all filled with writing. All of them had dates.

Wow!

This was her mom's old diary. Ellie had a chance to read it.

7

MOM'S WORDS

Ellie was not a big reader. But she read her mom's words deep into the night. The only light was from a candle.

June 15

Dear Diary,

Hooray! School is out! Not a minute too soon. I hated 9th grade. Hated, hated, hated

9th grade. The good part was lunch. And gym. My French teacher was mean. My English teacher was boring. My science teacher had a long hair in his ear.

One day, if I ever have a girl who says she doesn't like school? I hope I will read these words again. I get it.

Ellie smiled. She was not like her mom. She liked school a lot. She read on.

But there was one good thing. A new boy came to school today. His name is Colby. He is so fine. It is hard to look at him.

I don't have the guts to talk to him. The

year-end picnic was today. He came over to say hi. I couldn't speak!

I hope he's back next year. I would like to get to know him. Maybe something good will happen! I hope I have more guts in 10th grade. Time will tell.

Until next time,

Robin

Ellie's heart beat hard. She read the words again. Her dad's name was Colby. Her mom was Robin. Her mom and dad had met in high school. But she had no idea how it happened. These words were proof. Her mom had fallen hard for her dad. Her mom had been shy. It was sweet.

Colby + Robin = 4♥♥ Ever

"Hey," she said to Kate. "Check this out. You have to see this."

Kate was in bed. She looked bored. "Sure. It has to be better than what I'm doing."

"Which is?"

"Counting back from 600. By sixes."

600 594 **588** 582 576...

Kate came over. Ellie showed her the diary. "Isn't this cool?"

Kate shrugged. "Not so much to me. It seems so slow to write it by hand. But they didn't text back then. Poor dudes. I'm going to bed. See you in the morning. Maybe the power will be back on. I hope so."

Ellie watched the candle burn. She thought about what Kate had said. Yes. Writing was slow. Texting was faster. But if her mom had texted, the messages would be long gone. This diary? It had lasted a long time. It would be here many more years. Maybe Ellie's own kids could read it.

Cool, Ellie decided. Very, very cool.

8
THE COOKOUT

It was the next morning. Nana and Poppa woke the girls. "Good news!"

"What?" Ellie asked.

"It's the power. It's back on!" Kate cheered. "Yes."

"Not yet," Poppa said. "But half the state is good. We'll be on by midnight. We heard it on the radio."

Kate shook her hair out. "Thank God. Can I get the first shower?"

Ellie grinned. They had been washing in the ocean. "You don't like seawater?"

"Not much. Fish poo in the ocean," Kate said.

"I'm looking forward to fresh food," Nana told them. "The stuff in the fridge is about to go bad." She sighed. "Hate to throw it out."

"Maybe we don't have to," Ellie said. She had an idea. Her mom had met her dad at a picnic. So how about … "We must not be the only ones with food. How about a picnic? For the whole street. People can bring all the fresh food they have left. We can cook it up."

Nana smiled. "Poppa? What do you think?"

"We're in. If I don't have to do the invites."

Nana turned back to Ellie. "If you kids make it happen, we'll be there."

Ellie gulped. A picnic would be a lot of work. But it would be a fine way to end the blackout. Besides, her mom had met her dad at a picnic. Would she meet someone that way too?

The picnic was a hit.

Ellie and Kate had gone door to door. They had asked a ton of people to come. Most said yes. They all met at a nearby park. There were 100 people. Maybe more.

Poppa and the men made a fire. They

cooked hot dogs and burgers. Blankets were spread on the ground. Best of all, it had cooled down. The breeze felt great.

Everyone ate. Then a kickball game started. Kids against the grownups. Ellie was a good kicker. On the first ball, she kicked it to the fence.

"I'll get you for that!" shouted the pitcher. He was a cute boy her age.

"What's your name?" she called boldly. She had stopped at second base.

"Billy."

"Billy," she repeated. "You need to learn to pitch!"

Billy laughed. So did Ellie.

Ellie didn't think this could be the boy for her. But she knew one thing. She didn't need her smartphone to have fun.

9

THE NOTEBOOK

Homer was at the picnic. Ellie saw him standing alone. That made sense. He was an oddball. He had that crazy house. And his strange hobby. Still, he had helped her and Kate. She wanted to thank him again.

Thanks, Homer!

She went to him and said hi. "Thank you. For letting me talk to my parents."

"Hey," he told her. "Nice job on this picnic. I heard you made it happen."

Ellie smiled. "I had help."

A soft wind blew in off the ocean. Homer raised his face to it. "Can I tell you a secret?"

"Sure. I guess."

"When this is over? The blackout? I'll miss it. I haven't seen a picnic like this in forever. People are talking to each other. It's great. What about you? Will you miss it?"

Ellie looked out at the park. The kickball game was still on. She didn't remember the last time she had played kickball. Most of the time she would take pictures. Then she would post them.

Just then Homer took out a small camera. He snapped one shot of the game. Then he put the camera away.

"Just one?" Ellie asked.

"Sure. More is a waste."

"But you won't have the perfect one. I always take 10 or 20."

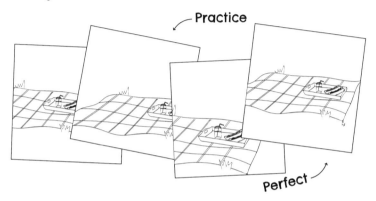

Practice

Perfect

Homer shrugged. "I don't need perfect. I just need good. If you're busy taking pics? You can't be in the moment. That's why I like my ham radio so much. You text a lot. Right?"

"Sure."

Homer looked at her. "How many kids can you text at once?"

Ellie thought about this. She'd texted

with 10 or 15 friends at once. "Wow, a lot."

Homer smiled. "The radio is easy. I only talk to one friend at a time."

He turned his eyes back to the game. Some kid kicked the ball into left field. There were many cheers. Homer cheered too.

Ellie didn't cheer. She was busy thinking. She liked being out here. There was a fun kickball game. Homer was easy to talk to. Yes, she wanted the power back on. But she also didn't want the blackout to end.

10
LIGHTS ON

The police stopped at every door. They said the power would be back on by nine. It was now eight. Ellie had found a blank notebook in the big trunk. It had a hard cover. The paper was green. Kate listened to the crystal radio. Ellie wrote. She used a candle for light.

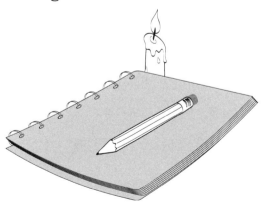

Dear Diary,

This is new for me. I never kept a diary before. I never wrote anything for fun. Some kids have blogs. This is no blog. Blogs are typed. This is handwritten. It will be slower to do. That's fine. Maybe slower is smarter.

I'm at my grandparents' house. They live at the beach. There is a blackout. I hated the blackout at first. I couldn't do what I wanted. I'm here with Kate. She's a great friend. But Kate hates the blackout so much. Now I kind of like it. It changed me.

I've learned a lot of stuff. I had no idea what a ham—

It happened so fast.

The lights came on. The water heater hummed. So did the fridge.

The power was on!

Kate cheered.

Ellie heard shouts from outside.

"Woo-hoo!" Kate danced around the room. "I can charge my phone. Free at last, free at last! Thank God."

Kate got her cell and plugged it into the charger. Ten seconds later, she powered it up. It beeped once. Twice. Then more. It kept beeping for almost a minute. "Wow. I have so many new texts!"

Ellie grinned. "Enjoy them."

"Don't you want to plug in?"

Ellie shook her head. "No rush. It can wait."

"I'll do it for you."

Kate found Ellie's phone. She plugged it into the wall. Then she turned on all the lights. Ellie didn't care. She was busy.

So the lights just came on. No big deal. I was talking about things I learned. Ham radio is cool. Crystal radios are cool. Kickball is cool. Even writing by hand is cool. I want to keep this diary for a long time. If you're reading this? That means you found it. Enjoy. It's my life for you to see. Know what? I hope you have a long blackout sometime too.

Until next time,

Ellie